THE LOST ONES

Margaret Greaves

THE LOST ONES

Illustrated by Honey de Lacey

DENT CHILDREN'S BOOKS
LONDON

Published in paperback in 1992
First published in hardback in 1991
Text copyright © Margaret Greaves, 1991
Illustrations copyright © Honey de Lacey, 1991

Printed in Great Britain by
The Guernsey Press Co. Ltd,
Guernsey, Channel Islands
for J. M. Dent & Sons Ltd
91 Clapham High Street
London SW4 7TA

For Jean, Tamsin and Zoe

Contents

Beyond the Door

The small princess was much younger than her sisters. When they were nearly grown-up she still had lessons with her governess, and very dull they were. When they were not having lessons she and her governess walked sedately in the palace gardens, where all the paths were straight and gravelled and all the flowers grew in neat rows just as they were told. Sometimes Deirdre saw glimpses of wild woods and fields beyond the palace gates, but when she asked to walk there her governess was cross.

'They are not safe,' she said sharply, 'and they would make your dress dirty. You should be happy to walk here in your own beautiful garden.'

Deirdre thought the garden would be more beautiful if even one of the paths had a curve in it, or a single tulip grew out of place. But she never said so.

She was happiest in her own small bedroom and

11

sitting-room at the top of the east tower, where sometimes she could be alone. Her sitting-room had three windows. From one she could see a great stretch of forest where trees tossed in the wind and little ragged bushes grew freely below them and the wild birds flew up in flocks. The second window looked towards a long range of mountains, so far away that they were sometimes no more than a blue shadow against the sky. The small princess watched them and wondered what it would be like to climb them and see what lay on the other side.

From the third window she saw the town spreading downwards from the palace to the farms and fields and gentle countryside. Beyond that, a glittering blue ribbon on sunshiny days, a misty grey one on cloudy days, and nothing but pale mist on rainy days, was the sea. The small princess had never been near the sea, but she thought it the most wonderful mystery of all. It had no barriers except the sky itself.

At long last she grew old enough to leave the palace schoolroom and join the older princesses.

'Now,' said the Queen, 'you are nearly grown-up. What would you like to do?'

'Oh please,' said Deirdre joyfully, 'may I walk in the forest beyond the palace gates?'

'*What*?' cried the Queen, shocked.

'No princess walks in a wild wood,' said the first princess. 'It would be most improper.'

'It would not be safe,' shuddered the second.

'Only a silly child would think of such a thing,' said the third princess scornfully.

The Queen gave orders that shutters should be put up over the window that looked towards the forest. Deirdre went sadly to her own room that night. She opened the door, then closed it quickly again with a little cry of fright and fled back down the stairs. The third princess was just then walking by.

'Whatever is the matter?' she asked.

'There's a lion in my room,' chattered Deirdre. 'A great big golden lion.'

'Nonsense,' said her sister. 'How could there be a lion in your room? Don't make up silly stories.'

She walked on, and Deirdre slowly climbed the stairs again. Perhaps she had only imagined the lion.

She opened her door carefully, and there he was. He was standing quite still and didn't seem to threaten her. He was very beautiful, golden as sand, with great golden eyes. Slowly she held out her hand and he touched it with his nose. He padded to the shuttered window and tore a great scratch down the wood, then back to the door as if he wanted her to follow.

'No,' said the small princess. 'They would be afraid of you down there. Together they would kill you.'

All that evening she sat beside the golden lion and stroked his fur and talked to him, and at last fell asleep with her head against his flank. In the morning she woke in her own bed and the lion had gone.

Now Deirdre watched the distant mountains more than ever, and longed to run on their slopes and feel the wind in her hair.

'Deirdre,' said the Queen one day, 'you are more grown-up now. What would you like to do?'

'Oh *please!*' cried Deirdre. 'I should like to ride

to the mountains and climb to the very top and see what is on the other side.'

'Are you mad?' demanded the Queen.

'No princess would dream of such behaviour!' said her eldest sister.

'Who knows what dangers may be there?' protested the second. 'Goblins, or dragons, or ghosts!'

'Stupid child,' scolded the third. 'When will you learn to be a proper princess?'

The Queen ordered shutters to close the window that looked towards the mountains. Very sadly the small princess went to her room that night. As she opened her door she saw the lion. He looked thinner, his golden hide seemed dull, and he paced to and fro as if the room were a cage. She threw her arms round his neck, and his purr rumbled like distant thunder. Then he shook her off and tore at the shuttered window, and padded to the door as if to get out.

'No, no,' said the small princess. 'I'm sure they would kill you down there.'

At that he lay down beside her, and their sadness flowed into each other until they found some comfort and fell asleep. But in the morning Deirdre woke in her own bed and the lion had gone.

After another while the Queen said, 'Surely you are now grown-up. What would you like to do?'

'I don't know,' said Deirdre. 'What do proper princesses do?'

'Nothing, of course,' said the first princess.

'But we do it very elegantly,' said the second.

'And we spend much time being beautiful,' said the third.

'Oh dear!' said the small princess desolately. ' I don't know how to do nothing. And I shall never, never be beautiful.'

She was quite right. All her sisters were tall and slim, with yellow hair and violet-blue eyes. Deirdre was short and plump, with tawny-brown hair. Her eyes were flecked with gold.

Sadly she went back to her own room. The lion was there. He was even thinner than before. His sand-gold fur was rubbed as if against the bars of a cage. When he saw the small princess he dropped his head on her feet, and golden tears ran from his golden eyes and down his beautiful broad nose. Deirdre threw her arms round his neck and her own tears fell into his mane.

'Wait!' she said at last. 'Wait. Don't leave me tonight. Let us wait until the palace is asleep.'

A long time they waited. The Queen and the three princesses went to bed. The servants washed the dishes, laid the tables, made up the kitchen fires, and at last went to bed too. The small princess opened her door and listened.

'Come,' she murmured, laying her hand on the lion's head.

Together they slipped through the open door and went lightly down the stairs. A curtain whispered in the darkness, falling ash settled softly in the dying fire. But no one heard or saw them as they passed. The drowsy sentries never knew when Deirdre drew back the bolts of the great entrance doors. A dog barked in the courtyard but no one heard it. The iron gates in the wall of the palace garden swung silently open to let them through. Side by side,

golden under the rising moon, they slipped through the edge of the forest and on towards the limitless sea.

'Whatever can have happened to Deirdre?' said the Queen next day.

'She's run away,' said the first princess.

'Just as well,' said the second. 'She would never have made a proper princess.'

'She *said* there was a lion in her room,' mused the third. 'Perhaps it has eaten her up.'

For many years after that there were strange reports from travellers abroad at night. Some said they had caught sight of a girl and a great beast wandering side by side through the forest, others had glimpsed them against the skyline of a mountain. Strangest of all were those who claimed they had seen them dancing with their own black shadows on the white and moonlit sands beside the sea. But as the Queen and the three elder princesses never went beyond the palace gardens they never heard any of the stories.

The Foundling

Janet set down her broom and listened. She could hear something else as well as the drip of the rain – a scratching, slithering sound as if a hand groped for the latch. Quickly she opened the door.

'Let me in! Let me in!' whined a voice outside.

It was the queerest thing she had ever seen, no taller than a child and with a child's face, yet wizened and sly. Its arms and legs were twig-thin, its tear-stained cheeks the colour of old oak leaves. Its eyes were the most startling thing of all, bright and piercing and as sharply green as spring grass.

Janet didn't like the looks of it at all, but it seemed distressed. It was also very wet.

'Come in, then,' she said. 'Get warm and dry.'

The thing flashed past her and curled itself up on the hearth, quick as a cat. It rubbed its hands at the fire and grinned at her.

'What's the trouble? Are you lost?' asked Janet.

The thing began to whimper again. It pulled up its ragged jacket and she saw the mark of a horse-shoe on its thigh as if it had been branded there.

'They left me,' it complained. 'There was cold iron on the pony and it kicked me. And then they all ran away. They didn't care. They left me all alone.'

Janet's heart beat faster. Only last week Farmer Gray had sworn that his poor old pony was fairy-ridden. He had asked the smith to shoe it again although it was out to grass. Only fairies and bad things fear cold iron. But the thing on her hearth was wet and hungry and cold and she couldn't bring herself to turn it out into the rain again. She ladled some warm broth into a bowl and broke some bread.

'Eat this to warm you while you get dry.'

The creature almost snatched the bowl, and ate hungrily, watching her sidelong out of its green eyes. Just as it finished, Janet's husband came home from work.

'What's this?' he asked sharply. 'Where have you come from? And what's your name?'

The creature gave its wide crooked grin and shook its head.

'Ah, that 'ud be telling.'

'It's an unchancy thing, whatever it is,' said Giles to his wife. 'You shouldn't have let it in. It must go.'

'Too late,' said Janet. 'It's eaten bread in our house. We can't turn it out now.'

The visitor looked from one to the other, sly and watchful, and wriggled closer to the fire.

'I'll do you no harm,' it promised. 'I like it here.'

Giles was troubled, but the bread of hospitality,

20

once given, left him no choice. So the thing stayed. Janet called it Brand because of the mark on its thigh. She even grew quite fond of it, but she took care that the neighbours shouldn't see it. If anyone glimpsed it at door or window she said her cousin's sick child was staying with her and must be kept quiet.

The visitor kept its word and did no harm in the house. But odd things happened outside. Farmer Gray's cows stampeded when they passed by in the lane. Dogs howled when they came near the cottage. A small whirlwind blew up the skirts of old ladies on their way to church, and Brand's grin was as wide as a sickle moon. The villagers became curious, and whispers of anger and suspicion began to reach Janet's ears. She wouldn't turn Brand out, lost and abandoned by his own kind as he was, but she was daily more worried. She felt too, that despite his tricks, Brand himself was secretly unhappy. At last she took him with her to visit the white witch who lived in the forest. The witch had helped many folk with her wisdom. Perhaps she could help even here.

The old woman was sitting at her door in the sun. She looked up as they came and clasped Brand's long skinny hand in hers.

'Come away in, my honey, come away in.' She smiled at Janet. 'There's trouble in two hearts here, I think.'

'I haven't got a heart,' flashed Brand.

He glinted at her out of his grass-green eyes, half-angry, half-afraid.

'That's your trouble,' said the white witch. She seemed to know all about him without being told.

'Your own kind have no hearts and you don't belong to the human kind. You live in two worlds and belong to neither.'

'Can you help us?' begged Janet. 'Is there no spell or charm for him?'

'No spell can create a heart,' said the witch. 'But perhaps he can make one for himself. If you can do three things out of mere love, Brand, you have some hope of becoming human.'

'My people do not know what love is,' said Brand.

'But *you* do,' said the white witch. 'You have seen it in Janet. Go home and try.'

Brand had expected magic and was sadly disappointed. He sulked all the way home, and was very naughty for a whole week. Even Janet lost patience with him.

'Horrid Janet! Cross Janet!' teased the creature, dancing and capering in front of her as she went to hang out her washing.

He tugged roughly at her sleeve so that she lost her grip of the basket and all the clothes fell out into the mud. Janet was very busy and very tired and the laundry was all to do again. It was too much. She burst into tears.

'Oh!' cried Brand, dismayed. 'I didn't mean it. Dear, kind Janet, I'm sorry. I'll do it again myself. Oh, please don't cry.'

And do it himself he did. He was only just tall enough to reach the washing-tub, and when he'd finished he was streaked with soapsuds and as wet as the day he first came.

Janet laughed at him, and then looked closer.

'You've changed,' she said. 'You're not so ugly

– not so very ugly. That was your first act of love.'

'Was it?' said Brand. 'I didn't know.'

Next day he watched the village children trooping into school.

'Janet,' he asked. 'If I grow human will I have to go to school?'

'Of course,' said Janet.

Brand was very quiet. He seemed to be thinking, and next day he was as naughty as ever. His tricks gave Janet a headache. But he was sorry when he saw how pale and tired she looked. It gave him a pain in his chest that he'd never felt before.

'You sit and rest,' he said. 'I'll get the supper ready.'

'Why, Brand!' exclaimed Janet. 'Your face looks almost like a real child's. This is your second act of love.'

'Is it? I didn't know,' said Brand. 'Janet, if I grow human and grow up, shall I have to work very hard all day, like Giles?'

'Of course,' said Janet.

Brand was very quiet all that evening. Next morning he said, 'I must go. I must see the white witch again all by myself. Goodbye, Janet.'

He was gone before she could say a word.

The white witch seemed to be expecting him.

'Come away in, my honey,' she said. 'I see something already human in your face.'

Brand burst into tears. He howled and stamped and looked as wicked as he had when first he came to the village.

'I don't *want* to be human,' he yelled. 'They'll shut me up in the schoolhouse all day long, and then make me work every day. I want to be free.'

'Hush, hush!' said the witch. 'Do you want to go back to your own kind then?'

'No,' howled the creature. 'They don't care about me. And they are old, so old, and they live for ever. And they would make me ugly again like them.'

The white witch held out her arms and drew him to her as if he were really a child.

'It's a cruel thing, little one, to be left between two worlds. And to know that you are ugly. You are too good for the fairy folk and too wild for humankind. We must find some other way for you that is beautiful and happy and free.'

All that day Janet waited and waited. Brand had said goodbye to her, but she hoped to see him again. She had grown fond of her tiresome visitor in spite of his tricks.

Just before sunset, a rapturous burst of song broke from the apple tree outside her door. Startled, Janet looked up. In the tree a golden-breasted bird with a scarlet crest flirted its wings and tail in impudent joy. It was pouring out its heart in music sweeter than a blackbird's. It paused for a second to look down at her with a bright and shining eye – an eye as vividly green as the grass in spring.

Ann Maitland

It was a cold, wet, miserable evening when the Maitlands invited us to stay the night. The rain had brought down a fall of earth on the railway line, and we should have had several hours to wait for the next train. We didn't want to give them so much trouble, but they insisted. They were kindly people, living in an old decaying family house far too big for them; and they said they would really enjoy having visitors.

'You can have Ann's room,' Mrs Maitland said to me. 'You won't mind, will you?'

She spoke as though I knew the name. I hadn't known them very long, so I didn't like to say that I remembered no mention of any Ann. In any case she must be away if I was to have her room. I said it would be very nice. Mrs Maitland looked slightly surprised.

It was indeed very nice. It was a quiet low-ceil-

inged room, overlooking the garden. I sat on a big oak chest in the window and looked out at the rain-soaked grass and tattered autumn flowerbeds. I thought how happy and friendly the room felt behind me. There was a child's book lying on the chest, that I thought I would look at later.

Someone had lit a small fire in the grate. The flames danced and flickered with such a welcome brightness that I preferred to sit by them without turning on the light as the evening closed in. Outside, the rain still fell in sullen sheets, drumming and sliding against the window. I sat with my back to it, not bothering to draw the curtains, and held my hands towards the blaze.

I don't know when I began to feel that I was not alone. But there came a moment when I was *certain* that someone else must have entered the room noiselessly without disturbing me. A sound other than the driving weather had gradually made itself noticed. I turned my head.

Curled up on the chest by the window, gazing out into the wet garden, a little girl sat and hummed to herself in a small sweet voice as quiet as the rain itself. The unknown Ann must have come home unexpectedly, and hadn't yet noticed that there was a visitor in her room. I spoke gently in order not to startle her too much.

'Is that you, Ann?' I said. 'I don't think they knew you were coming. I must be in your room by mistake.'

The child turned her head and looked at me. One hand still lay lightly on the book on the chest, the other went to her lips in a surprised movement. She looked fragile and bewildered. I wanted to soothe her, but felt suddenly unwilling to touch those delicate, almost transparent fingers. I spoke very gently.

'It's all right,' I said. 'I'm only a visitor.'

I got up and moved towards her. And suddenly there was nothing at all between me and the grey square of the window, nothing that blocked the view of the dripping garden and the blowing trees.

Startled, I reached for the bedside lamp and switched it on. The dark oak of the chest shone back at me with a soft gleam in the sudden pool of light. There was nothing there but the child's book. I picked it up and the cover fell open. All over the first page a name was written, again and again, in a round scrawled hand.

'Ann Maitland. Ann. Ann. Ann Maitland.'

A very young Ann had been practising her name. And in the bottom corner, in the same hand, was a date – 9th November 1840. The Ann who had owned that book had written on the flyleaf one hundred and fifty years ago.

Stranger from the Sea

A great wind was herding the horses of the sea.
It stampeded them against the cliffs, tossing wild
white manes of spray, and drove them thundering
and shouting all along the shore. Ned staggered
against the gale as he tramped homewards across the
beach. Among the seaweed and driftwood and
crushed shells of the high tide line he noticed a
broken creel.

'I'll take that home and mend it,' thought Ned,
stooping to pick it up.

But though the fishing basket was broken, it
wasn't empty. Curled up inside it was a baby, wearing nothing at all but a necklace of green beads. It
lay quite quiet and gazed up at Ned with sea-blue
eyes.

'How in the world did you get here?' cried Ned.
'You poor little thing, you must be starved with
cold.'

Being a kind-hearted lad he took off his own jersey and wrapped it round the strange little creature. Then he carefully picked up the creel, baby and all, and took it home to his mother.

Ned's mother was a widow, and found it hard enough to keep herself and her son. But she took the child in and cared for her; and when no one came forward to claim her she brought her up as her own. So Ned and Effie (as they called her) grew up together and loved each other.

Effie was never like the other girls in the village. She was fair-haired and pale and quiet. She learned to spin and cook and mend, but she would never walk far. She said the rough ground hurt her feet. In dry hot weather she seemed to wilt like a fading flower. But when the autumn rains and wind set in she was refreshed and lively again. Often she would sit at the window, listening to the heavy drops against the pane, but as if she waited for some other sound.

The cottage looked towards the wooded hills and not towards the restless sea, and Effie's foster-mother was glad of it. Sometimes, when the weather was wild, the roar of the waves carried like distant thunder even as far as the cottage; and then the girl would seem uneasy and would leave her needlework forgotten in her lap.

'It's no wonder,' said Ned's mother. 'She must be terrible a-feared of the sea, half-drowned as she was, poor lamb.'

She tried to protect Effie from the sight and sound of it, and if they went walking together it was always inland. Effie had only one reminder of her infancy, the necklace of green beads that she always wore. They were strange, pale, half-transparent things, that gleamed like raindrops in moonshine. Effie loved them.

One spring there came a grey, still day when Ned was down at the harbour and his mother had gone to market. Effie slipped out of the cottage and down to the shore. There were no fierce sea-horses that day. Only the little white sea-foals danced at the edge of the sand, their hooves striking out lacy patterns of foam.

'Look! Look there!' whinnied the smallest foal. 'The girl with the sea-green beads!'

The other foals rushed forward a little way.

'The beads!' called another. 'The magic beads. The beads of the Sea King's lost daughter!'

One after another they whinnied their message back to the swelling water behind them, past the near rocks, past the headland, out and below the deepest tide. Through the swaying forests of weed and the darting fishes, across the bleached sand of the ocean floor it ran, and into the Sea King's palace.

Ned was coming back from the harbour when he saw her, gliding like a sleep-walker towards the grey tossing sea.

'Effie! Effie!' he called. 'Come back. What are you doing here all alone? Come home. There's a storm brewing.'

The wind was indeed beginning to rise, and wicked little cat's-paws of foam ran over the darkening water. He put his arm round her and she came with him unresisting, but said never a word.

All day she was silent, and seemed hardly to hear

when they spoke to her. Ned had been right. With every hour the rising storm grew stronger. Even through the closed windows of the cottage the roar of the distant breakers made a constant murmur of sound.

When it was nearly dusk, Effie dropped her sewing and jumped suddenly to her feet.

'They're calling me,' she cried. 'Calling! Calling! I must go.'

Before they could stop her, she was out in the windy evening, running, running, to the sea.

Ned raced after her, shouting her name, but she fled all the faster. At last he caught her, almost at the edge of the tide.

'Effie, listen to me. Come home.'

Effie turned to face him, 'I am going home,' she said. 'This is where I belong. You and your mother have been good to me, Ned, and I will never forget you. But now I must go.'

'No, no!' pleaded Ned. 'Have you not been happy with us all these years? I had thought to marry you when you are older. I love you, Effie.'

'I love you, Ned. But it is no use. I know now who I am. I am not of your kind and there could be no peace in such a marriage. You will grow old but I shall never grow old. You will want comfort and a place by the warm fire, but I shall want the wild wind and the sea. You must marry a girl of your own kind, dear Ned, and be happy with her.'

'How can I be happy if you leave us?'

She reached up and kissed him, and her lips were cold as the flying spray. Her long fair hair blew out behind her like seaweed streaming in the water. All

34

along the beach the great sea-horses neighed and stamped and chafed until the solid earth seemed to tremble.

'It will happen one day,' said Effie. 'You will not forget me, but you will forget to grieve. Goodbye, dear Ned.'

A huge wave swept towards them, larger than all the rest. In the fast-fading winter light, Ned glimpsed the white tossing crest of a horse, its dark eyes gleaming. With a cry of joy Effie leaped on its back, turning its head towards the open sea. He saw her hand lifted in farewell, saw her toss something that fell at his feet, then saw no more than the great flying fountains of spray.

Ned stooped to see what she had thrown to him. At his feet gleamed a heap of pale green beads, the necklace of the Sea King's once-lost daughter.

Bracken

The November afternoon was closing in. It would be dark even earlier than usual. The distant damp murkiness was thickening and moving nearer. Very soon it would turn to fog.

Jenny shivered and began to hurry. It was two miles from the village to the farm where she was staying with her mother's friend while her parents were away. On a good day it was a lovely walk, across fields, through woodland, and then along the river bank. But today everything was bleak and cold. She had come out only because she was bored indoors, and now she began to regret it.

Mrs Purvis had suggested taking Berry with her, but Jenny had made an excuse and escaped without him. She didn't like to confess to his owner that she was terrified of dogs. Two or three years ago she had been attacked by a nervous, ill-trained retriever as big as herself, and she had a livid scar on her left arm. She wanted to be brave about dogs, but after that she couldn't. Berry, the black and white collie, seemed very big, and she kept as far away from him as she could. She did wish, though, that she had some human company. She was a town-dweller, unused to the emptiness of the darkening landscape.

She squelched across the first field and made for the broken bit of fence beside the wood. It was nearer that the stile and she wanted to get home quickly.

It was a mistake. Jenny didn't yet know the wood well enough. She walked downhill, thinking that would bring her to the path from the stile, but her way was soon blocked by a great patch of bramble. She skirted round it, then after a few yards came to a piece of boggy ground where coarse yellowing grass pushed up in hummocks that gave no sure foot-hold. Her boots sank in so far that she was nervous and backed out. The only firm path looked to her to be going in the wrong direction.

She stood still, wondering what to do. There was real fog round her now, moving stealthily in among the trees. The swirling coils of it suggested shadowy things that might be watching her. She was suddenly aware of the sounds that somehow made the stillness seem all the more still and uncanny. Somewhere out of sight a twig cracked. Something rustled beneath the withered undergrowth. Every now and then a heavy drop of water fell with a plop from a bare branch. Suddenly, with an abrupt clatter a partridge broke cover almost at her feet. Jenny cried out with shock and began to run down the path. She tripped over a fallen branch, nearly fell, clutched at the nearest tree, and stood gasping for breath.

It was then that she saw it.

A few yards ahead, another path crossed her own – and just beyond it crouched an enormous dog. He was black and white, rather like Berry, but brindled instead of patched, and much, much larger. He was crouching, head on paws, his muzzle pointing towards her, ears alertly erect, yellow eyes glowing.

Jenny stood absolutely still, paralysed by fright. Then step by step she backed away, keeping her eyes on him.

And he was no longer there!

She was sure she hadn't blinked or looked away, but the path ahead was empty. She waited a moment, her heart thumping. Then, when she was sure the dog wasn't there, she hurried forward to the crossing and took the way on the right. In the fog and the gathering dusk she could see only a yard or two ahead; but surely any path would lead somewhere out of the wood, and any was better than the one where the dog might be.

At a turn round a small clump of bushes he was there again! This time he was creeping towards her, belly almost flat to the ground. Jenny would have screamed but the sound froze in her throat. Blindly she turned and bolted back the way she had come.

This time chance was good to her. In her headlong panic she struck the path from the stile and in a very short distance was out of the wood and on the riverside track. For the first time she dared to look back. Nothing was following.

It was already the brief interval between evening and night. Bushes were only dark blurs, looming

through the fog like crouching beasts, and it was difficult to see the rough ground at her feet. Jenny had never felt so lonely or so frightened.

All at once he was there again – no longer threatening, but trotting quietly beside her. His tail was waving gently and he looked up at her with friendly eyes. Jenny stopped and he stopped beside her.

Suddenly she felt that any company was better than none. He didn't look so fierce after all. Timidly, very slowly, she held out her hand. The dog touched it briefly with a nose even colder than the fog. Encouraged, she bent to pat him, but he seemed to slip aside beneath her hand. When she walked on he was there again, detached, but still a friendly companion.

A murmur ahead of them became a rushing noise. They must be close to the weir. Almost immediately the track twisted and then divided into three. Jenny had only been that way once before, and now she was bewildered by the fog. Which track? Hesitantly, at last she chose the one in the middle.

The rush of the unseen weir had become almost a roar. She could feel the fine spray of it on her face, and the ground was muddy and slippery beneath her feet. She looked for the dog, but he wasn't there. Instead, there was a low threatening growl. Close in front of her, two eyes glowed luminously in the dark. Trembling now, she retreated, step by step, and the glowing eyes followed. She reached the division of the track again and this time chose the one on the left. The eyes disappeared as if someone had flicked off a torch.

Gasping, half-running, she stumbled ahead. The

noise of the weir grew more distant. She had somehow missed the river path and could only hope that this one went in the right direction.

Suddenly she heard voices not far off. She saw lights moving, people were calling her name.

'Jenny! Jenny!'

She shouted back, almost sobbing with relief, and a moment later was gathered into comforting arms.

'Oh my dear! Thank heaven you're safe! We've only just heard – the river's flooded by the weir. The path is under water, running fast. What made you take the upper track instead?'

'It wasn't me,' said Jenny. 'It was the dog.'

'The dog? What dog?'

'A big brindled sort of collie,' said Jenny. 'A bit like Berry, but bigger.'

'Like Berry!' said Mrs Purvis. Her voice sounded rather shaken. 'That sounds like old Bracken, Berry's father. He always loved our children and looked after them when they went out. We used to say he thought they were lambs – he shepherded them just like the sheep.'

In the darkness Jenny felt Berry's rough coat against her leg, his head pressing up under her hand.

'Perhaps he still likes children,' said Mrs Purvis. 'He was a lovely dog.'

Jenny's hand rumpled Berry's head as he sprang up at her to welcome her home. Whoever her strange guardian had been, he had saved her life. Berry was like him. He too could be her friend. And perhaps other dogs weren't really so dangerous after all?

Swing High, Swing Low

Melanie was growing tired. It was fun to stay for the first time in the great empty house where her uncle was caretaker, and to be shown all over it. But there seemed no end to the grand rooms.

'And this,' said Uncle Arthur, 'was Hester's room.'

Melanie stared as he opened yet another door. This one was different. It was a child's play-room. There was a rocking-horse in one corner, a small desk under the window. A toy-cupboard stood open, showing a jumble of things inside. They all looked rather old-fashioned. On the floor lay a big green ball, covered with small pictures of children in frilly dresses or knickerbocker suits, playing various games. The shiny surface was cracked and worn in places.

'It looks as if someone's just left it,' said Melanie.

'It's a sad story,' said Aunt Clara. 'Hester lived here more than a hundred years ago. One day she ran out to play in the garden and never came back. They searched and searched, but never found a sign of her or any clue about what could have happened.'

'Her parents left her room waiting for her, just as it was,' added Uncle Arthur, 'and it became a sort of tradition in the family. No one else has ever disturbed it.'

'Ugh! Creepy!' said Melanie.

After lunch she was free to explore the gardens. She went very quietly down the terrace steps and across the wide lawn. It was a hot, still, sunlit day, and it seemed wrong to break the silence. Everything was too big and imposing – the great house looming behind her, the stone urns, the flowerbeds where the late summer flowers hung their heavy heads in the drowsy air. The lawn ended in a tall clipped hedge, with an archway in the middle.

Melanie drew a sigh of relief as she slipped through it. This place was much more friendly. A path led into a small paved garden with a pool at its centre. More clipped hedges surrounded it, and through another archway she came into a half-wild area set with trees and shrubs. A swing hung temptingly from a branch of the biggest tree.

Melanie perched herself on the seat, gripped the ropes, and began to swing. Higher and faster she went till it felt like flying, and her own movement made a little breeze in the windless afternoon. At last she tired, rocked gently to a standstill, and went back to look at the pool. For a long time she lay on her stomach on the warm grey stone, watching the darting goldfish and the dragonflies skimming the water-lilies.

There was a rustle beyond the hedge, a whisper, the ghost of a laugh. Melanie sat up quickly. There was someone in the wild garden. She got up quietly, tiptoed to the archway, and peeped through. There was no one there. She ran and hunted between the trees, but still she was alone. She had just turned to leave when she noticed the swing. It was rocking gently to and fro, as if someone had only just left it . . .

'Aunt Clara,' asked Melanie at tea-time, 'are any other children allowed in the gardens?'

'My gracious, no,' said Aunt Clara. 'Why do you ask?'

'Oh, I don't know,' said Melanie carelessly. 'I just thought I heard someone. But I must have imagined it.'

As soon as she could next day, she went back to the wild garden. Of course there was no one there but herself and a whistling blackbird. Melanie climbed into the swing and sang to herself as she rushed through the air and the ground rose and fell beneath her.

After a while she went back to the pool. She sat, leaning on one hand, to look down into it. It lay smooth and bright as a mirror, and she could see her own face reflected. She watched it idly for a moment, then glanced away at the flash of a dragonfly. When she looked back there was another face beside hers in the water. A boy's face, thin and laughing. And now another, on the other side of her, as if someone was peering over her shoulder. Melanie gasped with shock, and a startled fish jumped and shattered the still water.

She leaped to her feet.

'Who are you? Who are you?'

No one answered. There was no one there.

'Don't be silly,' Melanie said severely to herself. 'Of course it was only leaf shadows.'

She didn't admit that there were no trees close to the pool which could have cast any shadow. She peeped through the archway at the swing. It was swaying quite gently. Someone laughed. Or was it only that whistling blackbird?

For the next three days Melanie avoided the garden. There were plenty of other things to do. But on the last evening of her stay she told herself not to be ridiculous. She crossed the lawn as the light was already fading into the green-scented dusk of high summer. The pool waited, quietly, harmlessly. She passed by it into the garden beyond.

She heard the creak of the rope as the swing rocked. She felt, even before she saw, that there were people there. A long-legged girl came smiling from behind a tree. In the failing light her hair seemed green as the dusk. Another leaned down from a branch with a little crowing laugh of welcome. The thin-faced boy was suddenly at her side. Out of the corner of her eye she saw others moving.

'We've been waiting for you,' said the thin-faced boy.

'For ever so long,' said one of the girls. 'It's been ages since we had someone like you to play with.'

'Catch-as-catch-can,' called another voice. 'Come on.'

A wave of happiness swept over Melanie. Whoever these people were she felt they were friends. She

47

laughed aloud and began to run, chasing and chased, between the trees, round to the pool, back to the trees again. At last, gasping for breath, she grabbed at the swing.

'Stop! Stop a minute!' she begged. 'I can't run any more.'

Her companions stopped. It was difficult to see them clearly. Some of them seemed almost like part of the trees.

'Who are you?' asked Melanie. 'Where do you come from?'

'We belong here, of course,' said one of them. 'We were here before the house was built.'

'Don't you know it's called Oakhill?' asked another. 'You know the rhyme.

> Fairy folk
> Do live in oak.'

'*Fairies?*' whispered Melanie.

'Maybe. Maybe not. But this land is ours. Stay with us, Melanie.'

'What do you mean?'

'You like us, don't you? Stay with us. Play with us. Stay! Stay!'

Melanie felt a confused sense of happiness and longing. The air seemed heavy with all the scents of summer, it trembled with bird calls. She held out her hands and other hands closed over them.

'She's ours! Ours!' exulted the thin-faced boy. 'Let's have another game. Here!'

Something bounced and rolled to her feet. She picked it up. It was a ball. There was just enough light left to show the little pictures that covered it.

It was smaller, but just like the one she had seen five days ago – a small ball made to match the big one in the deserted play-room. Fear froze her into stillness.

'It's *Hester's* ball!' she whispered. 'You! It was *you* who stole her away!'

'She was happy with us. So happy!' said one of the girls. 'You will be happy too, Melanie. Come!'

Once again her hands touched Melanie's. They were no longer warm, but cold and clinging as water-weeds. With a sharp cry Melanie turned and fled – through the arch, across the paved garden, over the lawn. For a few moments she felt herself pursued by shrill mocking calls and clutching hands that melted into air, but they followed no further than the pool.

At the foot of the terrace she stopped and looked back, a stitch in her side. Were those really dancing figures in the distance – or tree shadows moving in the light wind that comes just before dark? Was it chill laughter that she heard – or only the first owl-calls?

She hurried in and up to the sitting-room, glad to see that the lights were already switched on.

'Why, Melanie!' exclaimed Aunt Clara. 'You look as if you'd seen a ghost.'

'No, not a ghost,' said Melanie.

What was the use of trying to explain? It was more than a hundred years since Hester had played on the swing in the wild garden. There was no one to grieve for her now.

Friends

'All right, Mum. I won't be late.'

Alec shut the door behind him with a little stir of anticipation. The house removal was over, everything was more or less in place, and at last he was free to explore his new surroundings. They were a challenge to his sense of adventure. There was so much to find out, so many things to do. If only he could find someone to share the excitement! Alec was a lively person who loved company and he missed the friends he had left behind.

He took the lane away from the village, followed it past open fields, then climbed a stile into a wood. This seemed a good place to begin. It was quiet and peaceful under the trees, fallen leaves muffled his footsteps, and sunlight made sharp blades across the path.

Soon the trees opened out into a clearing. Here there was a small cottage that might once have been the home of a gamekeeper. But now it had an empty, abandoned look. There was no smoke from the chimney, no curtains at the windows. Grass grew high against an old sun-blistered door.

Alec went closer and walked all round it, noticing the cracked paint and broken sills, the cobwebs and dust that partly covered the windows. He peered through one of the panes and glimpsed a small bare room, with a table and a broken chair that someone hadn't bothered to take away.

He had just turned to go when, out of the corner of his eye, he caught a flicker of movement inside the house. So it wasn't empty after all! Alec stood still, embarrassed, wondering how to explain his curiosity. The pale blur came closer to the window. It was a face, a boy's face looking out, a cheeky, friendly sort of face. Alec gave a sigh of relief. It would be easier to talk to a boy of his own age than to apologise to grown-ups.

The boy had seen him. He grinned and waved, and Alec waved back. The boy was saying something, beckoning and pointing towards the door. Alec couldn't catch the words, but the gesture was clear. It was an invitation to go in. Alec hesitated, then knocked.

No one answered. But the strange boy's face pressed against the window. He beckoned again, then mimed the opening of a door.

It was odd that he didn't open it himself, thought Alec. Perhaps he was lame or crippled. But he was certainly telling his visitor to come in. Alec lifted the door latch and pushed. The door creaked, moved slightly, then stuck. A few flakes of paint fell off.

It was sagging on its hinges so that it scraped on the stone floor.

'It's too heavy. Pull a bit from your side,' called Alec.

The only answer was a laugh, and he got no help. Feeling a bit cross, he gave the door a hard shove with all his weight. It gave way very suddenly, with a rasping shriek of wood against stone, and he stumbled forward through the gap. The boy was waiting for him.

'You might have helped,' complained Alec.

'Yer didn't need it,' said the boy. He had a rough country voice. 'I'm right glad to see yer, though. I bin waiting long enough for some'un to come. D'yer live nearby?'

'We've just moved in to the house at the end of the village,' said Alec. 'This is my first chance to explore. I'm Alec Singleton.'

'I'm Barny,' said the boy.

Alec looked round the almost-empty room. Dust lay thickly on the table and the broken chair and dimmed the light from the small grimy windows. An old iron kettle stood on the hearth beside the ashes of a burned-out fire. He could hear no sound of anyone else moving about. He wondered hopefully if Barny was camping out. If they made friends, this could be a wonderful hide-out to share.

'Are you all on your own?' he asked.

Barny nodded.

'They've gone ahead with most of the stuff,' he said. 'Us be flitting. They'll be back for me later.'

'They? Do you mean your parents?'

'That's right.' Barny's cheerful face clouded for

a moment. Alec noticed that his features were peaked and thin as if he'd been ill. 'They bin gone a long time though.'

'Is it far you're moving?' asked Alec.

But the boy seemed not to hear him. He ran across to a corner where steep narrow stairs led up to a room above.

'Bet yer can't catch me,' he crowed, darting up them.

Alec followed at a run but wasn't quick enough. The stairs were broken here and there, and once he nearly lost his footing. Halfway up, the stairs turned sharply, each step narrowing to a point. He had to take this bit slowly. The room at the top was as bare as the other, and for a moment Alec thought it was empty. But suddenly Barny was there, coming out from a shadowy corner.

'A snail 'ud do better'n that,' he teased. 'After me now!'

He slipped past and down the stairs again as neatly as a mouse into its hole. Alec scrambled behind him, stumbling in the half-light. Barny grinned at him cockily.

'Not fair,' said Alec. 'You know those stairs and I don't. Anyway there's not much we can do here. Come on out.'

'No,' said Barny. 'No. I likes it 'ere.' He sounded stubborn and defensive. Alec was puzzled.

'But there's nothing to do,' he persisted. 'Oh, come on, Barny!'

'There b'ain't nothing outside neither. And it's cold out there. Stay wi' me and talk. Tell me where you be from.'

'No,' said Alec. 'This is my first chance to explore. We can't waste a good morning indoors. *You* come out and show me things.'

An odd secret look came over the boy's face.

'All right then. You go first.'

Glad to get his own way, Alec went out quickly, back to the path beyond the cottage. He expected Barny to follow, but there was no footstep behind him. Looking back, he saw him watching from the doorway.

'Hurry up!' called Alec.

Barny raised a hand as if to wave and took a step back. The shadow of the half-open door swallowed him from view.

'Oh, do stop messing about,' shouted Alec impatiently.

There was no answer. He ran back to the cottage. There was no one in the downstairs room. For a moment he stood at the bottom of the stairs, wondering what to do. He'd hoped he'd found a friend to share an adventure with, but now he felt cheated.

'I know you're up there,' he called. 'But I can't be bothered to play silly games. I'm going.'

Cross and disappointed, he went out into the wood again and made his way towards the village. A man was working on the hedge close to the stile.

'Morning,' he said, in a friendly way. 'You'll be the new young chap from Shaw's Cottage? Looking about a bit, are you?

'Yes,' said Alec. 'I've just been through the wood. Who lives at that funny old cottage in there?'

The man looked at him thoughtfully.

'B'ain't no one lives there,' he said. 'Not since

the tinkers squatted in it a year or two ago. They stayed a bit, till the lad took ill and died, and then they flitted.'

'The lad?' said Alec. 'What was his name, do you know?'

'Never knew it,' said the man. 'About your age, 'e was. As full of mischief as an egg's full of meat, but a nice enough lad. You'd 'ave liked 'im.'

'Yes,' said Alec slowly. 'Yes, I think I should have liked him – very much.'

The Hunting in Buckshorn Wood

Dickon paused on top of the hill, at the broken gap that led into Buckshorn Wood. This was the quickest way home; but it was already dusk, and no one went through the wood after dark. Dickon no longer believed the old stories about it, but he still remembered them.

People said it was once an elvish wood. There had been a pedlar who left Little Norton one night but never reached Under Norton, though his pack was found at the edge of the wood next day. And Dickon's own Great-Aunt Rachel had come drifting out between the trees one summer night and had never been quite the same again: indeed she had always seemed to him rather odd.

It was nonsense, of course. In any case, his father would be furious if he was late home yet again. Why should he avoid the place because of a lot of old wives' stories? He hummed loudly to himself as he turned into the narrow path that led downward between the trees. He wanted to whistle, but it would have seemed too loud and shrill in the stillness. The soft path silenced his footsteps, and soon his humming ceased as well. A pale blurred shape swooped past him, and he jumped nervously before he realised that it was only an owl.

Then the sounds began, rustles and little muted whisperings, and the crack of a twig. An unseen bramble caught his foot and he fell headlong. When he scrambled up he could swear he wasn't alone. He could see no one, but the gathering dusk felt crowded, as if scores of people pressed and jostled all around him. The whispering sounds grew louder. The path was overgrown and he was no longer sure of the way. Dickon turned and tried to go back to the entrance.

It was no good; he couldn't find it. It was almost dark now and the brambles seemed to catch at him on purpose and the trees brushed teasingly against him. Dickon stopped and tried to think, and at once all the sounds stopped too.

Then suddenly a voice spoke just behind him out of the dense shadows – a smooth, thin voice, thin as a chill wind and grey as beech bark.

'I think you are lost, young sir. Can I assist you?'

The tone seemed old-fashioned, formal and polite.

'Yes, please.' Dickon gave rather a shaky little laugh. 'It's silly really, because I can't have come far, but I can't find my way to the road.'

'Allow me to guide you,' said the voice.

Dickon hardly trusted it. It was too dark now to see anything but a taller, denser shadow that

moved out from the nearest trees, a vague cloaked form with a blurred, uncertain outline. But he couldn't get out alone, so he followed where the shadow led, though it seemed to him that they went downhill towards the lower meadows instead of up towards the road. And still the spaces seemed full of unseen people.

'Not many travellers come this way,' said the thin grey voice, making polite conversation. 'They don't like the stories.'

'Oh those!' said Dickon, sounding as brave as he could. 'Silly old wives' tales! I don't believe *them*.'

'Don't you?' said the voice, rather mockingly. 'Don't you, Dickon?'

The trees were fewer just there, and the pale light that comes just before moonrise flickered through them. Dickon looked up at the tall figure and caught a brief glimpse of a narrow, laughing face, brown as dead bracken.

At that moment a horn sounded, sweet and clear, from the crest of the hill and another answered – so far away that it seemed an echo. Dickon spun round. The distant trees seemed to move and toss against the skyline. There was laughter behind him like the crackle of dry leaves, but when he looked round again his guide had gone, melted away as if he were just another shadow. The crackling laughter was swallowed up in a new sound, a fierce drumming of windy hooves that seemed to shake the earth at his feet as they swept nearer, down from the top of the wood. Now the horn sounded again, high and clear, cold and sweet and terrible. A great gust rushed through the trees so that they leaned before it with streaming manes of leaves, and the hooves thundered downwards, louder and swifter.

With a cry of terror Dickon turned and ran, faster and faster, stumbling on roots and stones, gasping for breath, while behind him the whole wood seemed to charge in pursuit. Ahead of him now was the little mill-stream that marked the boundary between wood and meadow, but closer behind was the silver note of the horn. With a last desperate effort he threw himself forward, cleared the stream at a single jump, and ran on into the meadow. Halfway across it he stopped at last, breathless, unable to run a step further.

Suddenly he realised that the hunt had ceased. For a moment he thought he heard laughter, laughter, all over the hill, thin as the crackle of leaves, mocking and clear as a horn. But when he looked back the wood lay still, shadowy and peaceful: and all round him was the empty, unpeopled space of the meadow under the pale light of the stars.

The Living-Room

Outside, a sleety wind hissed over the sodden garden. Inside, Miss Maybury bustled round, sweeping and dusting. The shabby little house was already clean, but the work helped to warm her. She hated winter, and everything in her living-room had been chosen to remind her of summer – the rose-patterned curtains, the flowered cretonne on the armchair, the wallpaper with its design of blossoming trees and birds of mingled blue and yellow. She noted sadly that there was a badly faded patch on the cretonne.

The doorbell rang sharply. Peeping through the curtains, Miss Maybury saw that her caller was the boy from next door, and put down her duster. She was never too busy for Tom, whether his call was convenient or not. He was an adopted child of elderly foster parents, and she suspected that he was lonely. When he was smaller she had often mended his toys, and when he was bored she would find small jobs that he could share with her. He was an odd boy, she thought, with his thin, secretive face, and yet she liked him. Sometimes he seemed much older than his years. She was touched that he repaid her friendship with a protective manner as if she were the one who needed care. To him she must seem very old and frail.

Tom hurried quickly in, out of the bitter wind. Miss Maybury took her biscuit tin out of the cupboard.

'Help yourself, and sit by the fire a minute, Tom, while I finish dusting.'

'I like this place,' said Tom. 'It's pretty.'

'I must say, I like a bit of brightness in a living-room,' agreed Miss Maybury. 'Cheers me up in this weather. I wish it was always summer, don't you?'

'Why do you call it a living-room?' asked Tom. 'A living-room ought to be alive.'

'What a queer thing to say,' said Miss Maybury.

Tom grinned at her. Really, she thought, sometimes he looks *very* odd.

'If you want summer, you can have it,' he said.

She stared at him, puzzled. Then a noise behind her made her turn her head. It was a very peculiar sound, a sort of raucous call followed by a twitter. For a moment she thought that one of the birds on the wallpaper had moved. She blinked and told herself not to be silly.

A warm sweet scent drifted across the room on a puff of air. There were flowers in the room! Roses trailed all round the window, their silken colours soft and glowing with life. Sleet still flickered beyond the glass, but her whole room was warm and full of sun.

Indeed it was rather too full altogether. Flowers of spring and summer seemed to be blooming happily side by side, banks of daffodils and bright anemones and late summer poppies. Branches waved where the mantelpiece had been. Their pink cheerful blossoms were a little blurred. Blue and yellow birds darted or perched among them with a strange consort of harsh and musical sounds. One of them settled close to her, looking worried.

'Poor things,' said Tom. 'They don't quite know what they are – blue jays or canaries. So they don't really know what to sing.'

Miss Maybury stared at him, increasingly bewildered.

'Don't you like it?' he asked anxiously. 'You *said* you wanted summer.'

'I did. But I don't understand. It's all so strange.'

'Only because you aren't used to it,' Tom reassured her. 'And you can get rid of it when you want to. You only have to say "Go summer. Come, winter", and your room will be just as before. But before you say "Come, winter", you *must* make sure that everything's in its right place.'

The sun was deliciously warm, comforting her chilled bones. She wanted to stay in this strange garden and forget the cold and the sleet, but she was afraid. Tom looked thinner than ever, as if the light could almost shine through him, and she saw that though he stood in the full sun he cast no shadow.

'Tom! How did you do it? Who are you?'

'A thing adopted,' said Tom. 'Don't be nervous,

Miss Maybury. You've always been so kind to me and I just wanted to please you. I thought you'd like it.'

He was clearly disappointed, and had a lost, forlorn look that touched her.

'Of course I like it,' she said bravely. 'I love it.'

To make him happy again she strolled round the little garden, smelling the roses, touching the flowers, stroking the coloured birds that were tame as canaries. She noticed a small patch of faded anemones and picked them off so that they shouldn't spoil the others. In part she still wanted to stay, enjoying the scent and warmth and colour, but when she looked at Tom she felt a faint cold ripple of unease. He was not the lonely boy that she thought she knew. If he could do this, what else might he do? And would it always be good?

Suddenly she wanted the safety of her own familiar room, and at the same moment she heard the click of the garden gate. She remembered it was Wednesday and the time when the baker usually called. Whatever would he think if he looked through the window? In a sudden panic she cried the words of command.

'Go, summer. Come, winter.'

At once she was back in her ordinary room in the grey winter light. The baker left her loaf on the step as usual and went away whistling. Miss Maybury sank trembling into her armchair. Her finger caught in a torn bit of cloth, and she saw that there was now a hole where the faded anemones had been. Everything seemed normal except for a loud fluttering noise. A blue and yellow bird was scrabbling anxiously at the wallpaper. Tom stood beside her.

'I told you to make sure that everything was in place first,' he said reproachfully. 'It can't get back. Oh well, I suppose I'll have to keep it as a pet.'

He caught the bird gently and tucked it under his jacket. Miss Maybury looked at his face and knew that, however odd he was, she was still fond of him.

'Thank you, Tom,' she said rather breathlessly. 'You gave me a lovely surprise.'

But Tom had already gone.

The Dancers under the Hill

Strange things happened that year. It all began when a gale blew down the ancient oak tree on top of the small green hill. In its ruin the roots dragged up great quantities of earth, leaving a black open scar on the green turf.

Soon after that the stories began to spread. One man had heard some eerie music. Another reported strange lights and shadowy movements on the top of the hill. Perhaps the storm had disturbed something long forgotten in the dark earth. No one quite believed it, but people began to avoid the place, especially on moonless nights.

One warm May evening, pretty Jane Thirkin came home seeming half-asleep, her feet dancing softly as if to a tune that only she could hear. Next morning she was gone before anyone else was awake, and there was never a glimpse of her again.

On the morning of Midsummer Eve, Hetty Pearce

and her sister, Sue, were picking flowers along the lane.

'Listen!' said Hetty suddenly. 'Do you hear it?'

'Hear what?' asked Sue.

'The bells. The golden bells.'

'I can't hear them,' said Sue, frightened. 'We've got enough flowers. Let's go home now.'

All that day Hetty was absent-minded. Sometimes she didn't answer what was said, but always she seemed to be listening. She went to the Midsummer Dance that night. But when it was time to leave no one could find her.

That night and all next day they searched for her, Sue among the rest, calling and calling. Some went one way and some another but, when at last they gave up and gathered together, Sue was not among them. She too never came home.

There was sorrow and bewilderment in every house. For many months girls kept close to home and children were never allowed out alone, but no one else was lost. The neighbourhood thought they were free at last from whatever evil thing had stolen their daughters.

May Day came round again. Colin Saxton was repairing a broken hedge. He whistled as he worked, looking forward to the evening. It was his younger sister's birthday, and he hurried home as soon as he had finished.

'Where's Kirstie?' he asked as he greeted his mother.

'She's gone up to the farm for more milk. She won't be long.'

The farm was quite close, just at the top of the

lane. Minute after minute went by as they waited, but Kirstie didn't return. At last, with a cold dread in his heart, Colin went up to the farm himself. No one there had seen his sister. Only too soon they knew that she too had disappeared like Jane and Hetty and Sue.

Colin's anger and fear hardened into resolve. He was sure that the green hillock was somehow the source of their troubles. Next morning he climbed up to the ruined oak and looked long and hard at the mound and at a great boulder embedded in the earth, almost as high and wide as a door. After a while he gathered some dry broken branches and began to pile them close to the boulder. He had nearly finished when he heard a light footstep close by. A wrinkled old woman, dry and twisted as a thorn tree, was glinting at him out of sharp eyes that made him feel cold.

'What are you doing that for?' she asked. Her voice creaked as if she rarely used it.

'I'm gathering firewood for my mother,' said Colin boldly. 'But it's too much to carry. I'll bring a handcart to take it away tomorrow.'

He bent again to his task. She stared at him in silence and went by, and when he looked up there was no one there.

Colin went home and waited until dark. He had put a long iron nail in one pocket and an old broken horse-shoe in the other. He knew that all the Old Things – witches and warlocks, fairies and goblins – are mortally afraid of cold iron. In his dinner-bag he hid a bottle of water and some foul-smelling old rags. As the first stars came out he set off secretly for the hill, carrying a lighted candle inside a closed dark-lantern.

Quick and stealthy as a stoat he crept up to the old tree. Nothing moved on the hillside. Then from deep in the earth itself he caught the sound of music.

Now Colin acted swiftly. He pushed the dirty rags into his pile of wood, dampened the top branches with his bottle of water, then took out his lighted candle and placed it carefully against some dry grass at the bottom of the heap. The flame took hold, and a wisp of smoke floated up from the damp wood above it. Last of all he took the iron nail from his pocket and rapped it three times against the huge boulder.

'For good or ill, open!' he commanded.

The heavy stone began to move, swinging slowly inwards. Colin whipped through the opening and, before it could close, drove the nail deep into the earth beside it. The stone rolled back behind him, but stuck quivering against the iron nail that kept open a crack as wide as his fingers.

The music was louder now and a dim light shone from somewhere ahead. He walked towards it, feeling his way along a stone passage until it turned a corner. Cautiously he peered round it.

He was looking into a hall that blazed with light from a million jewels embedded in its walls. He could see no musicians, but richly-dressed people were dancing to a melody that nearly set his own feet tapping. Despite the splendour of their dress they seemed thin and misty, wavering like candle flames. But among them were four human figures, four faces that Colin knew. They too, danced, but as if asleep,

dreaming and trance-like, their eyes were open yet saw nothing. As they came close to him, Colin cried their names aloud.

There was instant silence and stillness.

Colin sprang forward, putting himself between the girls and their strange companions.

'It's him,' shrieked an eldritch voice. 'Him that I saw near the Door. I should have ill-wished him then.'

A deep angry murmur answered her, as if a huge swarm of bees had been disturbed.

'Run!' said Colin to the girls. 'Up the passage behind you.'

They stared at him with blank bewildered eyes, but Kirstie understood. She fled and the others followed. The dancers swept towards Colin, a menacing half-circle of bright cold eyes and long, thin, clawing hands.

At once he snatched the horse-shoe from his pocket and held it up. The creatures fell back with a wailing cry, crouching, cowering, covering their eyes as if from burning light. Colin turned and ran along the passage. Thin spirals of smoke were already creeping through the crack of the door. Reaching it, he dragged it open and pushed the girls through ahead of him.

Outside they were caught in a cloud of evil-smelling smoke. Colin caught his sister's hand and pulled her through it. Together they raced down the hill and the others followed blindly.

At last, gasping for breath, they stopped.

'They say that fairy creatures can't abide dirt or foul smells,' said Colin.

Pale against the dark sky, the smoke billowed over the hill. Through it and above it streamed shadowy shapes like a flock of startled birds, lamenting as they flew.

The hill was never troubled again, and Kirstie in time forgot the dancers. But though Jane and Hetty and Sue took up their old lives as before, they were never quite like other girls. Always they seemed to be listening.

The Watcher

The bell-chamber was a queer sort of place on a weekday morning. The huge bells hung still and silent – Jacob, Esther, Gloria, Paul, Matthew, Benedictus, Peter, Magnificat. There was something almost threatening in their quietness.

'I don't think I like it much,' said Jane.

Andrew wouldn't admit that he felt a bit odd too.

'It's an enormous view from here,' he said.

Jane joined him at the narrow slit window. Beneath them lay the village, and beyond it mile after mile of farmland divided at last by the river. It all looked grey and misty under the fall of rain.

'I expect it looked like this even in Amos Fair-weather's time,' said Andrew.

They had both stared, as often before, at the dusty memorial tablet at the foot of the tower steps.

In Grateful Memory of Amos Fairweather
Master Bellringer of this Parish
Died 19th April 1789
By his timely Warning he saved 137 Persons from
the great Flood on the 12th February 1786
His watchful Care discerned the Flood,
His Warning made it known.
His faithful Soul is now with God,
His loss is Ours alone.

'The river's pretty full *now*,' said Jane. 'But they didn't have weather forecasts to help them in those days.'

The sound of hammering stopped and their father's voice boomed up from the stone stairway below them. He had been replacing a damaged bracket supporting the rope handrail.

'All right, children. I've finished. Time to pack up.'

They were quite glad to go. They'd seen enough of the bell-chamber. But on a sudden impulse Jane leaned over, reaching through the wooden safety-cage to give a sharp rap against the side of little Matthew. The metal shell, dulled and darkened with age, vibrated in response. It gave out a sweet deep humming murmur that filled the space around them. They were both startled.

'What did you do that for?' demanded Andrew. He spoke almost in a whisper, as if afraid that someone might have been disturbed out of sleep.

'Just to see what happened, I suppose,' said Jane. But she too spoke quietly.

She looked back as they reached the door. She

thought for a moment a tall shadow moved across the cobwebbed gloom of the chamber. She grabbed at Andrew.

'Look!'

'What is it?'

There was nothing moving after all. But there seemed a denser patch of darkness in the dim corner where the light never reached. A thin spiral of ancient dust rose from the floor as if something had disturbed it. She knew that Andrew had seen it too, for she heard him catch his breath before he spoke.

'What are you babbling about? There's nothing to look at.'

Jane shivered. She hadn't noticed before that the bell-chamber was so cold. She tried to speak carelessly.

'I thought I saw someone. But of course it must have been a trick of the light. It's so creepy up here.'

'Silly!' said Andrew – though he too shivered as if suddenly chilled. 'You're potty! Come on, Dad's waiting for us.'

'Careful, Andrew!' warned their father's voice. 'Keep close to the right at the bottom of the next spiral. It's badly worn on the other side.'

Neither of them said so, but they were glad to get out into the grey damp air.

All that day it rained, as it had for days before. True to the forecast, the wind was strengthening too, rushing across the river flatland with a kind of shriek in the fiercest gusts.

Andrew and Jane went to bed at night without protest, bored by the tedious hours indoors.

Jane had been asleep for a long time when the

noise woke her. At first she hardly recognised it. It came in crashing chords of sound, cut off suddenly now and then in the more violent gusts of the gale. Now she knew what it was. Benedictus, the great tenor bell, was shouting across the storm.

She scrambled out of bed and ran out on to the landing, to find that everyone else was up too.

'It's a warning bell,' said their father. 'There's something wrong.' He ran to the window that looked down the valley. 'Put out that light so that I can see outside.'

Someone flicked off the switch, and the black square of window space grew paler, showing dim outlines of the world outside.

'No! Oh no!' gasped their father, unwilling to believe what he saw.

They all crowded behind him, peering over his shoulder. Their house stood high, at the top of the village, and from where they clustered they could see far down the river. At the utmost distance of vision, a thin moving line of whiteness crossed the surrounding dark. It was the bore, the tidal wave that swept up the estuary and for miles inland twice every twenty-four hours. But not like this.

'Look at the width of it,' said their father, and his voice sounded strange. 'The banks have broken.'

Above them the clamour of the great bell still went on. Lights appeared in houses all over the village and twinkled star-like from outlying farms and cottages.

'They've heard,' said their mother. 'They'll get out in time. Thank heaven, old Joe Ballinger must have seen it.' Joe Ballinger was the captain of the bellringers. 'Jane, help me get out all the spare blankets. Andrew, put on the kettle and turn on the fire. We may bring back visitors.'

Their father had already gone out to do what he could, and in a few minutes they followed him.

The line of white across the river was already much nearer. Its tossing heads of spray rose and fell like phantoms in the dark. From the church tower Benedictus clamoured on. Clang, clang, clang. Danger, danger, danger!

The main street was full of people, some of them scared and bewildered, clutching bags and suitcases, others looking for opportunities to help. The church doors stood wide open, sending out a welcoming flood of light. The vicar and his helpers were urging people in out of the rain. Jane and Andrew heard him echo their mother's words.

'Thank heaven Joe saw it in time to give warning.'

There was another sound now, beneath the constant drive of rain and wind, a distant menacing rumble that grew louder every moment. The bore was sweeping on up the river. It struck the lowest cottages, broke against them in a huge flurry of foam, and rushed on. Behind it, over the fields on either side of it, a dull glimmer showed that there was now a great sheet of water where minutes earlier there had been only grass. The doctor and district nurse were making a hurried check.

'Is everyone here from the river cottages? Morrisons, Ashleys, Mrs Bourne? Mrs Porter, is the baby all right? Good. Yes, I think everyone's here.'

'Might have been worse,' said one of the farmers. 'But if we'd had no warning there'd have been a tragedy.'

'Good old Joe, we've him to thank for it,' said the vicar. 'We can tell him to stop ringing now, everyone's safe.'

'I'll go,' offered Andrew.

As he hurried up the tower steps, the great bell checked, lost its rhythm, and began to falter. The ringer had stopped, and stroke by weaker stroke the bell was rocking itself back to silence. Andrew ducked through the low door of the ringing chamber.

'It's all right, Joe. Everyone's safe.'

Abruptly he stopped. The bell-rope swung to and fro as if someone had released it a few seconds before. But there was no one there at all. The place was cold and smelled musty as if long disused.

Andrew stared, numb with shock. Could Joe, for some strange reason, have gone up into the bell-chamber? He turned and forced himself to climb up the next three spirals.

The bell-chamber too was empty and locked as usual. He peered through the grimy half glass of the door. The place was full of shadows, but there was enough light from the stairway to show that there was no one there. Benedictus was still rocking gently, reflecting stealthy gleams of light from the dark cavern of his upturned mouth, and the air shook with the echo of his past shouting.

It was harder to turn his back on that shadowed empty space than to face it, and Andrew hurried down the worn stones at dangerous speed. The feeble electric bulb was flickering, affected by the storm, so that shadows jigged across the rough grey stone.

One of them grew suddenly larger, denser, seeming to block his way, and once again he felt that shock of cold.

Andrew slipped, clutching at the rope-rail, his heart thudding. Then the light above him burned steadily again.

There was no one on the stair, but his foot was poised just above the worn gap on the left. One more step would have sent him crashing down. It was perhaps a minute, but it seemed like ten, before he reached the bottom of the tower. It was good to be amongst people again.

'There's no one there,' he reported, rather unsteadily.

'But there must be,' protested the vicar. 'Perhaps he passed you on the way.'

'He couldn't,' said Andrew. 'There isn't room.'

'It couldn't have been Joe, vicar,' said someone. 'He's gone to his sister's for a day or two.'

Jane looked at the memorial tablet at the bottom of the tower. Someone must have rubbed and dusted it recently. It looked cleaner than when she had last seen it.

'Perhaps it was Amos Fairweather.' She laughed a little uneasily. 'Only of course it couldn't have been.' She looked at Andrew and stopped laughing. 'Of course it couldn't have been. Could it?'

Spring Tide

The day after the great storm was also the day of the big spring tide, the highest and lowest watermark of the whole year. After the fury of the night the sun rose from a brilliant sky, the wind had dropped to absolute calm. Rows of white breakers and the big piles of torn seaweed were the only reminders of the recent violence.

Mark whistled quietly to himself as he scrambled over the boulders beyond the low headland. There were very few times when they were uncovered by the sea and when it was possible to visit the little cave. It was hardly a cave really, just a small hollow worn by the waves beneath a shelf of over-hanging rock; but he had discovered it himself at the last spring tide and it was his very own secret. Red and green anemones shone like jewels in every crevice.

The sea had only just left it and the roof was still

damp and dripping. So small, so unexpected, he felt there was a touch of magic in it. After a few minutes he went out again into the hot sunshine and found a flat dry space to sit.

For a long time Mark sat there, half drowsy with the warmth, his eyes dazzled by the restless glitter of light on water. Then suddenly he sat up, surprised and alert.

A young woman was walking towards him from the sea.

But of course she couldn't have come from the sea! It was only a trick of the shimmering light. She must have been ahead of him and explored even further than he had. Now she was quite close, smiling down at him.

'Hello,' said Mark shyly.

'Good day to you,' said the girl. 'You have found my cave.'

'*Your* cave?' Mark was disappointed. 'I found it last year. I thought no one else knew about it.'

'No one else but me,' said the girl. 'It has been my cave for many, many years.'

There was something odd about her voice, a kind of murmur that reminded Mark of a sea-shell held close to the ear.

'You aren't all that old,' he protested. 'You can't have known it a *very* long time.'

The girl laughed and sat down beside him. She looked, as well as sounded, odd, he thought. Her fair hair hung long and free, and she was wearing a loose green dress that reminded him of the green seaweed clinging to the rocks. Her eyes seemed to change colour like the sea.

'Look in my face,' she said. 'How old do you think I am?'

It was a beautiful face and smooth as a child's. But for a moment he saw the network of a thousand wrinkles like a tracery of shadows beneath the skin. The strange eyes held his, drawing him deeper and deeper, until he seemed to be staring into some bottomless pool in the rocks. Then suddenly she let him go, and he knew that he was trembling.

'Who are you?' he asked fearfully. 'Where have you come from?'

'From Lyonnesse,' she said. 'Where else?'

'No. You can't have done!' Mark spoke loudly, as if trying to wake himself from a dream. 'Lyonnesse is only an old legend.'

She sighed. 'Is that what they say of it now? It is too long since I walked on the dry earth; but the great storm stirred the very depths of the sea last night and woke me. Tell me your legend.'

'Everyone knows it,' said Mark. 'They say there was once a beautiful land between Cornwall and the Scilly Isles, until the sea drowned it.'

'They say well then. But it is no legend.' She shielded her eyes as if the sun hurt them, then stood up and caught his hand. 'Come first into the cave, for the light is burning me. Then I will tell you the story.'

Mark winced at her touch, for it was like a band of ice around his wrist, but he sat with her, just inside the shadow of the little cave. Her voice, whispering like the sea, seemed all around him.

'After King Arthur's death there was great sadness in Britain. But in Lyonnesse the old ways still went on, with laughter and banquets and tournaments, and there was peace in the land. Until the day the sea rose.'

He shrank from her, afraid. He wanted to escape, but his body felt heavy as if with sleep as her voice flowed on.

'Out of a clear day it came. Great billows rolling in, smooth, green, unbroken till they shattered against castle walls and poured in cataracts along the streets. The watchmen ran to the steeples, tolling the bells to call people to them for refuge – until the sea engulfed the churches and rose into the bell-chambers, and only the waves swung the bells to and fro, tolling the end of lost Lyonnesse.'

Mark's dream-like trance was broken by the sudden slap of water against stone. The tide had turned, making noisy little rushes amongst the boulders. He sprang to his feet, backing away from her.

'If you were there, you were drowned too. What are you?'

She smiled at him, lightly, maliciously.

'Not a ghost. Not a woman. I am that Nimian whom Merlin loved.'

Nimian! Nimian the sorceress! Mark remembered the story. It was she who enticed the great wizard Merlin into a cave, and then by her spells had enclosed him for ever in the rock. Suddenly he felt how small was the cave in which they stood, and how mocking and cold were her eyes. Fear gave strength to his will. He pushed violently past her, out into the sunshine and space.

Nimian laughed.

'He was an old man and he pestered me. I was

weary of him. But you need not be so afraid. I am the ancient magic of Lyonnesse – and, whether men heed it or not, old magic still lives on.'

Her hands reached out as if to draw him. The tide was almost at his feet, threatening his return. Yet, despite himself, he moved towards her. As the wave withdrew, sliding back off the rock, a hundred small voices whispered and hissed in its foam, 'Lyonnesse. Lyonnesse.' The sunlight poured over the paleness of her hair, her ageless young-old face, and glittered in her eyes. Suddenly she was not there at all, as if dissolved into the sparkling light.

The sea rushed closer, more noisily. The breakers were still heavy after the night's storm. Between them, as they rose and fell, Mark heard far off the faint drowned tolling of a steeple bell.

ALSO IN PAPERBACK FROM DENT

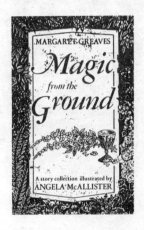

"These simple stories vibrate long-forgotten chords in the dark recesses of the subconscious."

Junior Bookshelf

Twelve stories to weave a spell of ancient charms and magic. An old man flies to the Mountains of the Moon and back, a miller becomes invisible and a child who sees the Little People is never seen again by mortal eyes.

Strange and incredible things happen between the pages of this book and all because of the remarkable powers of plants.